Can't Reach the Itch

by Joe Larke
Illustrated by Karol Larke

FIRST EDITION

To order additional copies write to:
GRIN-A-BIT COMPANY
P.O. BOX 235
ROCKWALL, TEXAS 75087

Published by GRIN-A-BIT COMPANY,
Rockwall, Texas
Printed by Taylor Publishing Company, Dallas, Texas
Helen Lance, Publication Consultant

ISBN 0-9620112-1-5

Preface

When I was young, poetry was not one of my favorite types of reading. In fact, I didn't read much of anything. So why am I writing poetry today? I like to write, and I like to read what I write. And I figure if *I* like it, you might, too.

Actually, children are my inspiration for writing. Their response to my first book, *The Bullfrog and the Grasshopper and Other "Tails"* was, "we want another book!" And here it is.

I trust *Can't Reach the Itch* will help poetry reading become more enjoyable and even create an interest for both children and adults to write poems for themselves. That's how I began. It seems that everyday situations have a unique way of recalling fond memories for all of us, regardless of our age. When you locate the poems that remind you of you, immediately you'll know I know we know that you can't help but "GRIN A BIT!"

Contents

Can't Reach the Itch 6

Black Toast 7

The Stuff You Don't Read 7

All Tangled in a Rope 8

Get Mad 9

That Tree Was Green 10

How Can I Know? 10

What's a Giraffe? 11

Zeke 12

A Mouse in Our House 13

A Bird and a Worm 14

Black Sock Sleeves 14

No One Can Tell It 15

I Wonder What 16

The Blades on My Fan 17

Peep and See 17

Riding in the Dark 18

My Life's a Drag 19

Slurp Slurp 19

Little Lost Dog 20

Not Bites! Bits 22

Back to Gold 23

Waiting for a Doctor 24

Hey 26

Horse Water to a Goat 27

My Sister 27

The Middle 28

My Uncle 29

The Pants I Wore 30

Beenee, Weenee and Deenee 31

Upset 32

My Old Lawn Mower 33

If We Were More Thankful 34

A Deal is a Deal 34

Chicken Biddy 35
Dropping a Hint 36
Here Came That Ball 37
Bad Mistake..38
James Lied 38
I Could Have Done Better...39
Bug in My Bed 40
Pic and Pac 42
Hate, Late and Wait 42
Unsquare Pairs 43
Grandma Dipped Snuff 44
Parts of a Tree 46
Disgusted 47
Red Horn-Rimmed Glasses..48
Boat with No Sail 50
Never Ever 50
Can't Blame It All...51
My New Dobb..52
Ceristalida 53
Black Ink 54
To Get to the Top 55
Cream Gravy..56
An Aspirin Bottle 57
Thoughts 58
Struggling 60
The Blind Man 62
Sybil 64
There Ain't No Choice..66
The Mind 68
This Ode's to Me 69
Alphabetical Index 70

Can't Reach the Itch

Why bother to scratch
When we can't reach the itch.
It's a loss of time
Trying something in which
There's no relief —
Only wasted motion.
So where do you get
That itching "lotion"?

Black Toast

My toast is black,
It got too hot.
I have to eat
Black toast a lot.
It could be better,
Haven't had any yet,
'Cause burned black toast
Is all I get.

The Stuff You Don't Read

Don't dare throw away
The stuff you don't read.
As soon as you do,
That's when you'll need
To read about something
You need to know.
But you-know-what-you-need
Is gone with that throw.

All Tangled in a Rope

I got myself
All tangled in a rope,
So I yelled to my friend,
Neighbor "Dopie Dope."
After one quick whiff
I knew he wasn't using soap,
And when my face wrinkled up,
He left me tangled in the rope.

Get Mad

Go ahead — get mad.
Your temper will sizzle.
What makes it bad,
Your character will fizzle.
You'll lose all control
When you're all upset,
'Cause things that should happen
Either don't or haven't yet.

That Tree Was Green

Two weeks ago that tree was green,
That's what the gardener said.
Today I'm looking at that tree
And it is solid red.

How Can I Know?

How can I know when I know what you know?
There's no way to know when I know what you know.
I'll bet when I know what you know it will show
On your face that I know what you know — then I'll know.

What's a Giraffe?

My gardener thinks
A giraffe is a bug.
Hunters all think it's a deer.
My carpetman says
He knows it's a rug.
Ranchers all say it's a steer.

My laundryman says
He thinks it's some soap.
My mechanic is sure it's a car.
Cowboys are saying
It must be a rope.
Weathermen claim it's a star.

Some policemen I know
Say it's a gun.
Pilots are sure it's a jet.
Firemen all say
They think it's a ladder.
Electricians say — TV set.

So I asked my dog "Tinker"
If she might know
What a giraffe could be?
She thought for a moment
And said, "I sure do.
A giraffe is a sore knee."

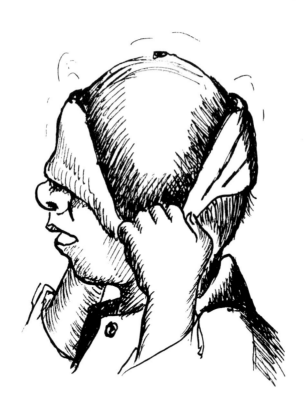

Zeke

Zeke pulled his cap
Down over his head
To cover up his fears,
He feels a lot safer
But doesn't believe
Anything else that he hears.

A Mouse in Our House

There's a mouse
In our house
Who lives in our den.
We never
Have seen him
Just where he has been.
It won't be
Much longer
'Til we see that there mouse,
'Cause he's eaten
Most everything
In the den in our house.

A Bird and a Worm

See that bird over there on the pole?
He's looking down at a worm in a hole.
The worm isn't worried in the least for his soul.
He's making faces at the bird on the pole.

Not a sound's been heard from the pole to the hole.
And nothing's been heard from the hole to the pole.
The bird flew down to pull the worm from the hole,
But the worm left a note — I'm over at the pole!

Black Sock Sleeves

My socks got twisted
With a shirt in the washer.
Now my socks are sleeves for my shirt.
But that's okay,
I can wear them longer.
Black sock sleeves won't show dirt.

No One Can Tell It

No one can tell it
Like Jamie's grandpa.
And no one believes it
Like Jamie's grandma.
He's told it so much
She's convinced that it's true.
I know that it isn't
But I'm believing it, too.

I Wonder What

I like a boy,
He doesn't me.
I'm nice to him,
He's not to me.
I wonder what
It could possibly be
He likes about her
And not about me?

The Blades on My Fan

The blades on my fan spin one way,
But look like they're going the other.
I know that they shouldn't,
The fan must be broke.
So I'm trading it in for another.

Peep and See

I opened my eyes
To peep and see
What I saw
Looking at me.

Riding in the Dark

I rode my trike
While my friend rode his bike
As we peddled our way to the park.
Our parents let us go,
But they said, "You must know
What will happen if you come home after dark."

We were having such fun
We forgot about the sun,
'Til it slipped behind the trees and out of sight.
Now we're riding in the dark
As we peddle from the park,
Thinkin' what will happen at home tonight.

My Life's a Drag

My life's a drag,
I sure get bored.
I don't do things
I can't afford.

Some say I should
I think so, too.
The friends I have
That's what *they* do.

Slurp Slurp

I dropped an egg
On the kitchen floor.
It spread underneath
The pantry door.
I heard "Slurp Slurp,"
Then tried to poke
What ate the white
But left the yoke.

Little Lost Dog

I was walking through the woods
On an old cow trail
When I saw a boy sitting on a log.
There were tears in his eyes
As he tried to explain
He was looking for his little lost dog.

He said it left his home
In the middle of the night
And he doesn't know where his dog could be.
I said to this young fellow,
"If you want to find your dog,
Climb off that log. Let's go, you follow me."

While searching through the woods
We heard a whining noise,
We found it, looked, and this is what we saw:
Fourteen little puppies
So young they could not see,
Laying with their mama on some straw.

The boy got real excited
'Cause we found his little dog,
And we watched all her puppies try to crawl.
He shook my hand and thanked me
For helping find his dog.
Now he knows she wasn't lost at all.

Not Bites! Bits

Two bites! Four bites!
Not bites, bits.
The pep squad yells
Like the ball team hits.

The girls didn't know
The words to the yell,
And the team didn't block
Or tackle very well.

It surely is proof
When you take away the fun,
The students won't like it
And nothing gets done.

Back to Gold

My fish is blue.
It got too cold.
Just yesterday
That fish was gold.

It cannot swim.
There's a smile on my cat.
My fish needs help
From his pal, the rat.

Oh! There he goes,
His pal, the rat.
It caught the eye
Of my smiling cat.

My fish looks good.
He is not cold.
Instead of blue,
He's back to gold.

Waiting for a Doctor

I'm waiting for a doctor.
I'm filled with fear.
I am not sick,
So why am I here?

Everybody's staring,
Looking right at me.
What in the world
Could the problem be?

I don't need glasses.
I haven't been hurt.
I don't hear well —
My ears are full of dirt.

Bones aren't broken.
I don't see blood.
I am a little messy —
Been playing in the mud.

But I do kinda itch.
There's a lot of speckles.
My friends all say
I'm growing freckles.

Said a lady in white,
"We're ready for you.
First door on the left,
Room number two."

A doctor came in
With a nose like a fox.
He said, "The reason you're here —
You've got the CHICKEN POX!"

Hey

Two boys walking.
One said, "Hey!"
The other, looking off, said,
"What'd you say?"

"I said, deaf ears,
You owe me some pay."
"You didn't, and I don't!
I heard you say 'Hey'."

Horse Water to a Goat

When your boat has a hole
In the bottom, it will sink.
When your horse isn't thirsty,
He will not drink.
So plug that hole
That's leaking in the boat.
And the horse that won't drink —
Give his water to a goat.

My Sister

I'm meeting my sister for lunch.
Our guest for the meal is her mother.
My sister, whose mother has only one son,
Knows her mom's son is her brother.

The Middle

You know the beginning
Doesn't start in the middle
And the middle isn't where the end ends.
The middle comes after
The end of the beginning
And precedes the beginning of the end.

My Uncle

I remember back when
I was a kid
My uncle did the plowing with mules.
When the plow broke down
I would be sent
To the barnyard to get him some tools.

His hands were so big
He couldn't hold small things
And everything got in his way.
I used to get tickled
At how he would fumble
Those tools and the words he would say!

But he was a farmer
And no one was better
'Cause crops that he raised were the best.
I loved my dear uncle,
Was always around him,
And must have at times been a pest.

I know that he loved me,
He told me he did.
He taught me a lot that I know.
And when he got ready
To go in to town,
He would always ask, "Where is my Joe?"

My uncle is gone now,
I really do miss him.
He surely was "special" to me.
But he left me with memories
Of our times together,
And when you saw him you'd see me.

The Pants I Wore

I was all dressed up
And hurrying to meet
My date for the night,
Who wanted to eat
In a plush little place
That was different but neat,
And things had gone well
'Til I saw my friend Pete.

As we passed Pete's place
He began to beat
With his fists on the table
And the floor with his feet.
He laughed so loud
It annoyed the elite,
'Cause the pants that I wore
Had a hole in the seat.

Beenee, Weenee and Deenee

Beenee, Weenee and Deenee
Are puppies that all look the same.
No one knows one from the other
And each has a sound-alike name.

Deenee's the two brothers' sister.
Beenee and Weenee are the boys.
When all are asleep and laying real still,
Everyone thinks they are toys.

Upset

I got up
When I got upset.
I got upset
When I didn't get
What's really mine
That I don't have yet.
So I'm still up
And still upset.

My Old Lawn Mower

I tried to start
My old lawn mower,
When I pulled on the rope it broke.
I got that fixed,
Started it up,
And all it did was smoke.

It spit and sputtered
And then it died.
I twisted on every screw.
I pulled and jerked
On the rope again,
Whatever I did, didn't do!

So then I thought,
"It needs a new plug."
I drove ten miles for another.
When I got back
And put it in,
It worked no better than the other.

I don't know where
I got this mower
Nor what brand name it is.
But whoever built
This piece of junk,
I wish it still was his!

If We Were More Thankful

If we were more thankful
For what we've got,
We'd have more compassion
For those that have not.
We can't have it all,
And money won't buy
The happiness we want.
Don't waste it and try.

A Deal is a Deal

A deal is a deal.
Either good or bad.
When it isn't any good,
Someone's mad.

But honor your word.
What you said — stick to it.
Follow through with your part —
You made a deal to do it.

Chicken Biddy

A chicken biddy hopped
And hopped
And hopped
And then,
It hopped some more.

It continued to hop
And hop
And hop
Until
It couldn't hop any more.

PLOP.

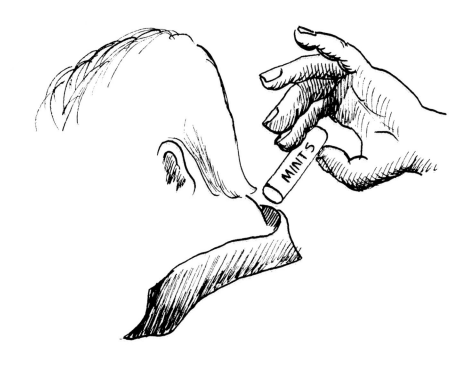

Dropping a Hint

What is your method
In dropping a hint
To a friend who's in need
Of a fresh breath mint?

You know that it's nothing
Of which he's aware.
So when you don't do it,
Are you being unfair?

Here Came That Ball

I could not see
When the ball was hit,
'Cause everybody stood
While I had to sit.
Here came that ball
Hit hard by the bat,
'Couldn't believe it was fallin'
Right where I was at.
Well, I caught that ball
In my cold drink cup.
Now everyone's sitting
While I'm standing up.

Bad Mistake

His daddy said, "Mow!"
His mamma said, "Rake!"
Either one he fails to do
Will be a bad mistake!

James Lied

James lied, then denied that he cried.
He told some things that weren't true.
He thought what he said
Wouldn't be read,
And never thought what might hurt who.

I Could Have Done Better

I've had a lotta fun
Standing right up here,
But I've been distracted
By a lady in the rear.

When I looked her way
She would always be
In the midst of a smile
And a wink at me.

If you didn't like things
Said as they were,
I could have done better
Had it not been for her!

Bug in My Bed

There's a bug in my bed
Under the sheet,
Snoring so loud I can't sleep.
It must be a big one
To make so much noise.
How shall I handle this creep?

I'm afraid if I move
It will waken the bug,
And make him so mad he might bite.
I'll do some quick magic
While jerking the sheet,
And "Shazaam" that loud bug out of sight.

WOW! That quick magic
Is really great stuff.
I wondered if it'd work like I read.
It did — I feel better.
I've turned out the light.
Now — What's that I hear in my bed!!?

Pic and Pac

Pic said, "Pac,
Scratch my back."
Pac said, "Pic,
Sounds like trick."
Pic said, "Pac,
Pic feel sick."
Pac said, "Pic
MUST be sick
If Pic thinks Pac
Scratch his back!"

Hate, Late and Wait

If Hate, Late and Wait
Called Fate to take a vacation,
In only one day,
The whole USA
Would evolve from a dying nation.

Unsquare Pairs

I made a box.
It was unsquare.
I tried another.
Have an unsquare pair.

They are not neat.
But no one cares.
Now I'm getting rich
Selling unsquare pairs.

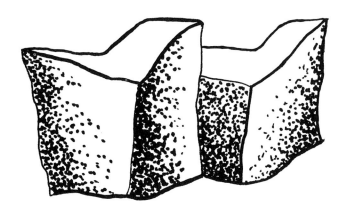

Grandma Dipped Snuff

I recall that my grandma dipped snuff.
She said it was bad tasting stuff.
She dipped and she spit
But would never admit
She never could quite get enough.

I remember I thought it was dumb,
But I asked her if I could try some.
My dipping was brief
As I cried for relief.
My mouth stung so bad it was numb.

How could my grandma endure
Something that smelled like a sewer?
But that stuff had a way
Of making her day.
So why she dipped snuff, I'm not sure.

Parts of a Tree

I remember when I was in school
And learning the parts of a tree.
I had a mind like a goose
'Cause it wouldn't produce
The parts of a tree for me.

It seemed such a poor use of time.
And why did I have to know
A branch from a stem
And a stem from a limb,
Or the roots on the trunk below?

One thing I never did learn.
When was a tree a tree?
Some were so tall,
While others quite small,
And how did they come to be?

Why did some grow so fast
While others grow so slow?
From a stem to a limb
Or a branch to a stem,
I know I still know I don't know.

HOLE

TRUNK

BRANCH

LIMB

SKUNK

STEM

ROOT

LEAF

46

Disgusted

I know why I
Am not asleep.
I'm wide awake,
Disgusted.

I got caught speeding,
Paid the fine,
Now my wallet's.
Busted.

Red Horn-Rimmed Glasses

Sammy wears red horn-rimmed glasses.
He really gets teased a bunch.
Five bullies are gathered and waiting
For Sammy to finish his lunch.

Out on the school yard they push him.
They trip him — he falls to the ground.
He tries to get up and they push him again,
The bullies keep knocking him down.

His glasses are stepped on and broken.
He really must have them to see.
He wonders why bullies are big boys,
Thinks, "Why are they picking on me?"

Sammy rises and dusts off his breeches,
Then kneels down to put on a shoe.
He's scared and he's mad and he's shaking,
But he knows what he's got to do.

Quickly, he's up and he's swinging.
He's spoiling the big bullies fun.
He's bruising the faces of three of the five
While the others are fast on the run.

In an eyeblink the action is over.
Sammy won and he's feeling quite proud.
When he reached for his broken rimmed glasses
He hears a loud cheer from the crowd.

So, never let red horn-rimmed glasses
Influence you to think someone's weak.
It could get you involved in deep trouble
For misjudging a size or physique!

Boat with No Sail

A boat with no sail
Is like a duck with no feet,
A lamp with no bulb
And a chair with no seat,
A table without legs,
A shoe with no sole,
A nest without eggs,
Or a sink with no hole.
But a sail on that boat
And a wind that will blow,
Will do what it couldn't
A moment ago.

Never Ever

When you try to do it to it,
It will take some time to do it,
For it never, ever has been done before.
But if and when you do it,
Yell and tell the world you did it.
You may never, ever do it anymore.

Can't Blame It All

The child is mad
And terribly bad.
He cries for things
He's already had.

He is not becoming
A very nice lad.
And we can't blame it all
On his mom and dad.

My New Dobb

I bought a new dobb.
It's a very good dobber.
In fact, it does all of my dobbing.
It's great for my sob.
It works well with by sobber.
And no one can tell I've been sobbing.

Ceristalida

Ceristalida is a very old chicken.
She constantly gets lost on the farm.
Her chicken pals know
Where she is and they go
To watch her and guard her from harm.

Ceristalida is "grandma" to the chickens.
She has taught every chicken to scratch.
She's shown them three ways
To scratch on rainy days,
And she starts every chic as they hatch.

The chickens dearly love Ceristalida.
She knows all their don'ts and their do's.
But her teaching career
In a "chicken" atmosphere
Is over — she bought her some shoes.

Black Ink

I'm using black ink
Rather than brown
Or yellow or pink or red.
It's easier to read,
And will not smear
Like using black pencil lead.

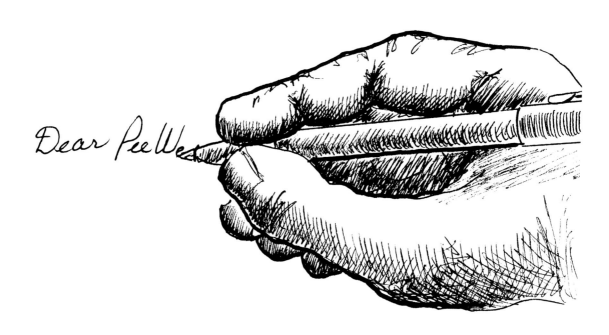

To Get to the Top

His father said,
"To get to the top
You're constantly stepping on toes.
To be somebody
In corporate life,
It's something that every one knows."

Regardless of what
You say or you do,
You do it to be number one.
Then once you have made it
You have no free time,
And working is no longer fun.

Everyone wants
A piece of your time
But there isn't enough in a day
To see all the people
Who want to see you,
And hear what they have to say.

The joy is all gone.
It's pressure and meetings
And ulcers and nothin's the same.
And all of those people
You stepped on to get there
Are helping you ruin your name.

Cream Gravy

Mom was in the kitchen
Cooking our supper
When the lights in the house went out.
It was "pitch black" dark.
We couldn't find the candles,
So none of us could see to move about.

She was cooking cream gravy,
Had flour in the skillet,
Then reached for the milk to pour in.
But since she couldn't see,
She grabbed the vinegar bottle,
And the odor wrapped our nose 'round our chin.

Mom never tried again
Cooking in the dark.
My sis and I were happy as could be.
Now when we're all at home
And cream gravy's on the table,
I look at mom — and Sissy looks at me.

An Aspirin Bottle

An aspirin bottle is giving him fits
He can't get the lid undone.
He thinks to himself, "This is the pits.
Ninety-five pills, and I can't get ONE!"

The label says, "Push and pull right here,"
And that's just what he did.
He got real mad the pills were near,
But he couldn't pop the lid.

He began to shout and stomp around,
Then rammed his fist through a door.
The lid popped off — the pills spilled out
And rolled through a hole in the floor.

Thoughts

Thoughts are more than nothing.
They can't be touched or seen.
Every brain creates it's own —
That's what makes them keen.

They stay inside the human mind
Until they're used or told.
Every thought has shape and size,
But can't be bought or sold.

They can be secret throughout life.
No one may ever know.
If they're kept within the mind,
They will never show.

So allow yourself some time to think.
It's therapy for the brain.
And any thought you don't want known,
The mind's where they'll remain.

Struggling

I'm in this math class
All confused.
Absurd that I am here.
I haven't plans
To be a doctor
Nor an engineer.

There's no desire
To fly a plane
Or navigate a boat.
The luck I have,
The plane would fall,
The boat would sink — not float.

Memory work
Just blows my mind,
I find it all too rough.
So why am I sitting
In this class,
Struggling with this stuff?

I don't intend
To get involved
In space flights to the moon.
So, the faster I
Get out of here,
Won't be a day too soon!

The Blind Man

"Well," said the blind man,
"I guess no one can hear.
I sing my songs and shake my can
But no one has come near.

"It doesn't appear to by my day,
My collections will be small.
Many times it's been this way.
Then times, no money at all.

"I have no legs. I cannot walk.
I travel on a cart.
I just wish someone would talk
And ease my lonesome heart.

"I live my life one day at a time,
Nothing to look forward to.
No eyes, no legs, and not a dime,
But still I sing for you.

"I hear those who pass me by
Talking as they go,
I sit alone and wonder why
They do not say, 'Hello.'

"It breaks my heart, I cannot play
The songs they'd pay to hear.
So many times I've heard them say,
'He's terrible — don't go near.'

"So if you think you have it tough,
Sit one day for me,
And listen to that awful stuff
They say 'cause I can't see.

"Then pretend you cannot walk.
Now, what do you do?
You cannot see . . . you want to talk
But no one talks to you.

"You'll wish so badly you could cry
To ease your lonesome heart.
And all the while you wonder why
You live upon a cart.

"There's got to be a reason why
God put me on this earth,
To live like this and bear the pain
I've carried since my birth.

"So, surely, there's a better day
Somewhere down the road.
Please, dear God, send one this way
To help me bear my load."

Sybil

The Civil War was not a war
That many thought was civil.
Those who served, shot and killed
Left many behind like Sybil.

She lost her mother and her dad
While trying to protect the farm.
She didn't know the soldier came
To do them any harm.

Her mom and dad were both shot down,
The soldier watched her cry.
As he marched away he said,
"I'll let you starve to die."

Another soldier coming through
Thought he heard a moan.
He looked around and there was Sybil
Dirty and alone.

It touched his heart as he thought,
"What a price to pay.
When people do not get along,
Live and die this way."

The soldier stooped and picked her up,
Then squeezed her to his chest.
He walked toward a big oak tree,
To sit and get some rest.

With a dirty face and stringy hair
She said, "I'm only three."
She stroked his beard and then said, "Mister,
Will you stay with me?"

There Ain't No Choice

I ain't got time
To go to school,
I gotta find me a job.
I don't have nothin'
And I sure gotta eat,
But I ain't gonna join no mob.

I wanna do somethin' —
I don't know what —
There ain't much I can be.
I'm having trouble
Finding work.
Nobody cares about me.

I try ever' day —
Ain't done no good.
I'm a drag to the community.
There ain't no choice
But to get back in school
And learn myself a degree.

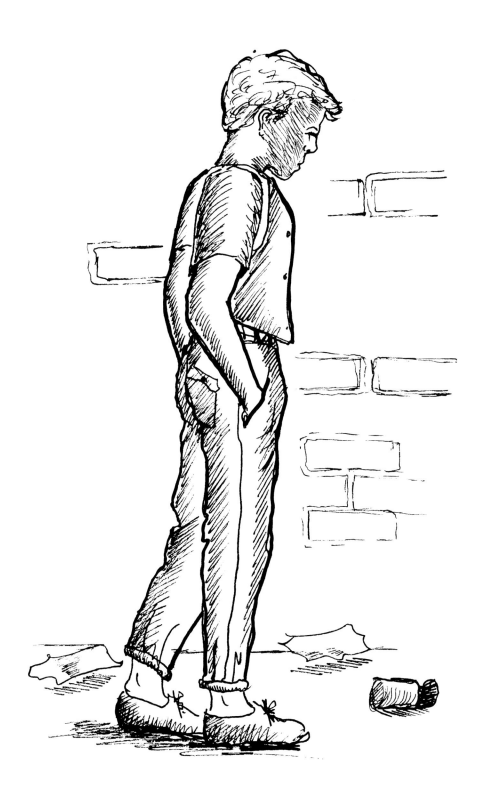

The Mind

The mind is a very complicated maze.
It produces amazing things.
It calculates and evaluates
Decisions the brain-maze brings.

It exercises complete control
While producing the things being sought.
Nothing compares to the mind when it's used
For placing in order each thought.

What seems to be missing are people who try
To think for themselves and to find
Ways to do better, be smarter and wiser
And not be left mentally behind.

This Ode's to Me

This ode's to me
Of whom I think a lot
About who I am
And how I got what I've got.
They said I had
What it takes to be great,
But no one had
The time to wait.

Now they're all gone
And it's just me,
Enjoying the fame
They wanted to see.
I wish those folks
Were still around
To see I did not
Let them down.

Index

All Tangled in a Rope 8

An Aspirin Bottle 57

Back to Gold 23

Bad Mistake...38

Beenee, Weenee and Deenee 31

A Bird and a Worm...14

Black Ink 54

Black Sock Sleeves 14

Black Toast...7

The Blades on My Fan 17

The Blind Man 62

Boat with No Sail 50

Bug in My Bed 40

Can't Blame It All...51

Can't Reach the Itch 6

Ceristalida 53

Chicken Biddy 35

Cream Gravy...56

A Deal is a Deal 34

Disgusted 47

Dropping a Hint 36

Get Mad...9

Grandma Dipped Snuff 44

Hate, Late and Wait 42

Here Came That Ball...37

Hey 26

Horse Water to a Goat 27

How Can I Know? 10

I Could Have Done Better...39

If We Were More Thankful 34

I Wonder What 16

James Lied 38

Little Lost Dog 20
The Middle...28
The Mind 68
A Mouse in Our House 13
My Life's a Drag 19
My New Dobb 52
My Old Lawn Mower 33
My Sister 27
My Uncle 29
Never Ever 50
No One Can Tell It 15
Not Bites! Bits..22
The Pants I Wore...30
Parts of a Tree 46
Peep and See 17
Pic and Pac 42
Red Horn-Rimmed Glasses....................................48
Riding in the Dark 18
Slurp Slurp 19
Struggling...60
The Stuff You Don't Read 7
Sybil 64
That Tree Was Green..10
There Ain't No Choice...66
This Ode's to Me 69
Thoughts 58
To Get to the Top 55
Unsquare Pairs 43
Upset...32
Waiting for a Doctor 24
What's a Giraffe?...11
Zeke 12

HUH!

I thought I wrote
A poem; I didn't.
So one I thought
Was in here, idn't.
Sorry.